Raccoon River Kids
The Second Adventure

EXTRAVAGANZA
AT THE PLAZA

by Lauren L. Wohl
illustrated by Mark Tuchman

ISBN: 978-1-943978-31-1

Printed in Canada

Library of Congress Cataloging-in-
Publication Data available.

10 9 8 7 6 5 4 3 2 1

Published by

PERSNICKETY
PRESS

120A North Salem Street
Apex, NC 27502
www.Persnickety-Press.com

CPSIA Tracking Label Information:
Production Location: Friesens Corporation,
Altona, Manitoba, Canada
Production Date: 6/15/2018
Cohort: Batch No. 244542

For Arlene and Paul,

Jeff, Julie,

Caitlin, Hannah and Brady,

Jodi, Jack

Mia, Gabriela and Tristan –

Your friendship is the inspiration.

1.

Scripting a Story

Hannah and Nico were riding their bikes past the old abandoned Plaza Theater in downtown Raccoon River. Its windows were painted black, its ticket booth was tattered and leaning, and its marquee spelled out some message with so many missing letters, you couldn't even read it.

"What do you think it says?" Hannah asked.

Nico read: "FAY UN"

Hannah tried: "F. A. space space space Y. space space U. N."

"That's what I said, Hannah. FAY UN."

They laughed.

"Come on. Let's figure it out," said Hannah. "U.N. That could be bun, sun, run, fun. What else?"

"I think it's FUN," Nico decided.

"Okay. FUN. Now the first word. F. A. space space space Y. What's that?"

They stared at the letters. It suddenly came to Hannah. "It's FAMILY. F. A. M. I. L. Y. It says, 'family fun.' Maybe there was a show here for the whole family. A concert? A movie? Something."

"Family fun," Nico repeated.

"I think that's something Raccoon River could use a whole lot more of," said Hannah.

"You're right," Nico said. "Like movies. We shouldn't

have to go into Franklin or to Middleton every time we want to see a movie."

"And sometimes we get there, and all the tickets are sold out. That's the worst," Hannah said.

The two friends thought some more. "We even have to go to Franklin for our graduations," Hannah said.

"Raccoon River graduations should be right here," Nico said.

"Right here. At the Plaza."

They stared at the theater, sure they were right.

"It isn't fair that our town doesn't have its own theater," Hannah said as she climbed up on her bicycle. "But maybe it could . . ."

2.

Two Questions

Little by little, day by day, Hannah's "maybe" grew into an idea. Or at least the start of one.

She took a brand-new red-and-white polka-dot notebook from her desk drawer, grabbed her favorite pen, and started writing.

THE RACCOON RIVER FAMILY FUN THEATER

Below that she wrote:

Opening Valentine's Day

That was five months away. Enough time, Hannah thought. She read the words aloud to herself a few times.

Yes, this was just what Raccoon River needed, and Valentine's Day was the perfect time to open. Absolutely!

Hannah turned to a clean page in the notebook and wrote down her ideas. On another page she began a list of questions.

By the end of the weekend, she had more questions than ideas. Hard questions. Could this project that was bubbling up inside her ever actually happen?

She looked over her list, but stopped after the first two questions.

1. Who owns the Plaza Theater?
2. Are there any rules about fixing it up?

Until she knew the answers to those questions, the rest of them didn't matter. Now who could help her find the answers?

"Can you drive me to school this morning, Mom? I need to get there early."

Her mother didn't ask why.

Hannah continued. "I have a research question I hope Mr. Fredericks can help me with."

"Okay, Han. I'll wrap up your breakfast so you can finish it in the car."

"Thanks, Mom."

Hannah looked at the clock when they got to school. The first bell would ring in twenty-five minutes. That was plenty of time for Mr. Fredericks to help her with two questions.

"Good morning, Hannah," the librarian greeted her. "You're bright and early. Is there anything I can help you with?"

"Two questions."

"Okay. Shoot."

"How do I find out who owns the old Plaza Theater?"

"And?" Mr. Fredericks prompted.

"And . . ." Hannah paused. "And, what do I have to do to get it fixed up? I mean, are there rules?"

Mr. Fredericks looked at Hannah. "Let's dig into that," he said.

3.

A Plan Is Brewing

Mr. Fredericks fired up one of the computers. While it was waking up from the weekend, he headed to the reference section. He reached up to grab a couple of over-sized books from the top shelf, then held them out for Hannah to see.

"We can find some historical information in this one. And there's a lot of information about renovation of public spaces in this other one."

"They're big! I bet they're pretty complicated too," said Hannah.

"I bet you're right, Hannah."

The computer sounded its opening tone. Mr.

Fredericks typed Plaza Theater, Raccoon River, Massachusetts.

The screen filled with articles and photos from the county historical society website.

Hannah took her notebook and starting writing. From the long list of facts, she copied:

Opened in November 1967

Built by the town of Raccoon River with taxpayer funds and donations

Seats: 350

Planned uses: movies, live theater, concerts, lectures, graduations, town celebrations…

Hannah underlined movies and graduations.

Architect: Sig Associates

Contractor: Cliff Contracting

Mayor: Stanley Levin

"Hah," Hannah said. "Stanley Levin was my great

uncle. I knew he was mayor once."

There were so many things to check out on the website, including more programs and posters than Hannah had ever imagined.

One of the programs stood out: Extravaganza at the Plaza.

"Wow. So much happened in the Plaza! What do you think this Extravaganza was?" Hannah asked Mr. Fredericks.

"Something spectacular, I guess."

"We could use something spectacular," said Hannah.

"The Plaza has been closed for twelve years," Hannah continued sadly. "It must be getting pretty dusty and dirty. It must miss all the excitement. I think all of us miss it too."

"It sounds to me like you've got a plan brewing," Mr. Fredericks guessed.

"Could be," Hannah answered.

The school bell rang. "Gotta' go. Thank you, Mr. Fredericks."

"What about these books?" the librarian asked, pointing to the large volumes he had left on a table.

"I'll need them. But not yet."

"Okay then. You know where they are."

"Absolutely," Hannah said and waved goodbye.

Nico was already at his desk when Hannah came running into class. As she walked past him, she whispered, "I've got something BIG to talk to you about. At lunch today, okay?"

Nico nodded.

In the cafeteria, they took seats at a small table in the corner, so no one would hear their conversation.

"Remember the theater?" Hannah asked.

"The Plaza?"

"We should fix it up. Open it up. Bring back Family Fun. Don't you think?" Hannah whispered.

"That's big, Hannah. Giant. Tons of money," Nico paused. "It sure is a great idea though."

"I almost have a plan, Nico," Hannah said softly. "After school?"

"Deal."

4.

Two More Questions

"Two questions," Nico said the moment he and Hannah left the school grounds.

"What are they?"

"First: how do we get inside the theater? It has to be locked up tight." Nico took a breath.

"And dangerous. But we have to see what it's like in there, don't we?"

"We do, and I don't know how," Hannah confessed.

"Second: how much is this going to cost?"

Hannah knew that question was coming: "We'll get people to donate," she answered.

"Do you think people will just give us all that

money?"

"They should. We NEED a theater. And we need more than money. People can donate their talents too. We need painters and plumbers, and . . . and . . . more. I have a list. It's long.

"But you're right," Hannah went on. "First thing, we have to get inside to see what kind of shape it's in."

"We can't just walk in," Nico said. "There could be alarms. And what if we get in and chunks of the ceiling start crashing down on our heads? We could get hurt. Who knows what's living in there? Not to mention that our parents would ground us till forever if we went there alone."

Hannah was thinking exactly the same things. She sighed. "I want to do something good for our town. I want us kids to do it. Like you did, Nico, with the playground. But this just might be too big."

"Are you giving up already?"

"It's not just getting into the Plaza that's a problem," said Hannah. "Mr. Fredericks showed me a gigantic book of town rules. This could be way too complicated for us."

"Probably is," Nico agreed. "It isn't something we could ever do on our own, even if every single kid in town helps. We need the grown-ups."

Nico watched Hannah's face. He knew how much she wanted the kids to do it all. But Hannah was agreeing.

"Of course," she said.

"Well then, if adults are going to be part of this, I think we can do it."

"I'm not so sure," Hannah admitted, "but we could take the first step at least and have a look inside the Plaza."

"Right!"

"So, we're back to how do we get in," said Hannah.

"My dad always says to start at the top," Nico answered.

"The top?" Hannah asked.

"The mayor! He told us we could come to him with our ideas for making Raccoon River a better place," Nico reminded her.

"He did," Hannah remembered.

"Let's call him."

"Are we ready?" Hannah asked, sounding worried.

"We better be, if you want the theater open on Valentine's Day," Nico said.

"Let's call."

Hannah and Nico walked to Nico's house. Melissa, Nico's older sister was in the kitchen. She didn't look happy. She took three glasses out of the cupboard, banged them on the counter, grabbed the milk from the fridge, poured it, then put the container back and slammed the door closed.

The three of them sat down on high stools. For a long while, no one said a word. Then Hannah said, "Are you okay, Lissa?"

"Nope."

That was not enough of an answer for Hannah.

"What happened?"

"You know I'm in the orchestra at school, right?"

Hannah and Nico nodded.

"We are putting together a spring concert. I got a solo part."

"That's great," said Nico.

Melissa turned to her brother. "Do I look happy about it?"

Nico shook his head.

"It would be great, if there was someplace where we could perform. Someplace that had room for more than just the students. Someplace where families and neighbors and maybe even some strangers could attend. A real concert."

"What about the high school auditorium? Could you use that?"

"It's not much bigger than the middle school's. The only place in Raccoon River that's large enough is the outdoor theater in the park. But the concert is in March, to celebrate the start of spring. It will be too cold."

"Maybe there's a place in Franklin or in the city."

"Too far," was all Melissa said. She stood up, put the glasses in the sink, and headed out of the kitchen. It was clear this conversation was over.

Hannah and Nico went to his room. They'd no sooner gotten there than Hannah said, "The Plaza. That would be the perfect spot for Melissa's concert."

Nico nodded. "Yes, it would be."

Nico took Mayor Wilson's card from the bulletin board on his closet door and held it up for Hannah to see. "Now we *have to* get the Plaza into shape."

"We sure do! What are you waiting for, Nico? Call the mayor."

5.

The Big Call

A woman answered. "Mayor Wilson's office. How can I be of assistance?"

Nico took a deep swallow. He was having trouble getting the words out. Finally, he found his voice.

"Hello. I am Nicholas Preston. I am Raccoon River's Top Businessman of the Year. The mayor said I should call him if I had an idea for our town. My friend Hannah has a great idea."

"Nicholas. Yes, I remember. You're the blueberry boy."

"Kinda," Nico answered.

"Nice to meet you, Nicholas. Let me see if the mayor is available."

He was. In a minute, he picked up the phone.

"Nicholas, it's good to hear from you. What's up?"

Hannah leaned into the speaker. "We have an idea for the Plaza Theater."

"Is that you, Hannah?" the mayor asked.

"It is. Hello."

"Now what about the Plaza? It's such an eyesore!" the mayor sighed.

"Uh-huh," Hannah agreed. "But it doesn't have to be. I have a plan."

"Interesting. What can I do?"

"Plenty."

"How about I come to your school tomorrow to talk?"

Hannah didn't know how to answer.

"That's it then," Mayor Wilson said. "I'll see you tomorrow. It's third grade, right?"

"Yes."

The mayor clicked off.

Just as he said, the mayor showed up at school Tuesday morning. He did his usual mayor-type stuff— shaking hands with the kids in the class, asking what they were studying, throwing out a hard spelling word. At last he asked if Nico and Hannah could be excused for a few minutes for "an official town meeting."

The three of them sat at a table in the library. The more Hannah told him about her plans, the more excited the mayor seemed to get.

The mayor had two questions of his own. "Do you know who owns the building? And is it sound...structurally stable?"

Hannah was ready for the first question. "The town owns it."

"Really? That's great. We won't have to buy it. I'll check with the building department. They should have been inspecting it every three years. They'll know its condition."

"When?" Hannah asked.

"Soon," the mayor said.

Hannah pushed. "How soon?"

"I'll make some calls this afternoon. Meanwhile, don't you think we ought to have a look?"

We? Hannah wondered, but she said, "Yes."

"Let's do that," the mayor continued. "How about Saturday morning? I'll meet you at 9:30 in the Plaza parking lot."

"We'll be there," Hannah answered quickly.

Hannah's backpack was stuffed to the max with an extra-large, extra-bright (and extra- heavy!) flashlight, an emergency lantern that the family kept in the garage in case of a storm, her polka-dot notebook, and a couple of pencils. She wore an old, messed-up hoodie and jeans.

Her backpack weighed so much that it kept slipping from her shoulders. Her bike teetered from side to side. It took twice as long as usual to peddle from her house to Nico's.

Nico was waiting outside. The friends rode to Main Street, straight to the theater. They were early. They wanted to get there before the mayor arrived, to check things out.

Nico went around the left side of the building, looking for a way in. Hannah took the right, pedaling very slowly, stopping to see if that basement widow over there was open just a little bit (it wasn't), or if the next one was loose in its frame (it wasn't), or if the door—"Stage Door" it said—was unlocked. It was!

"Nico!" Hannah shouted.

Nico gave the door a pull. It moved, but not a lot. The hinges were rusty and bent in places.

"It's stuck," said Nico.

"Let's try together," Hannah suggested.

They both grabbed the metal handle and pulled together.

CRASH! Nico jumped. "Whoa!"

The handle pulled off and fell to the pavement.

"Shhh," said Hannah.

They heard a car pull into the lot. It was the mayor, right on time. They hurried to meet him.

Mayor Wilson looked around. "I thought your parents would be here," he said.

Hannah answered quickly. "They said it would be okay as long as you were with us."

"You're sure? We could wait for them."

Hannah nodded. "We're sure."

"Okey-dokey."

Mayor Wilson handed Hannah and Nico yellow hard

hats. "Best to wear these." He put one on too, and Hannah led him to the Stage Door. The three of them pulled at the door. It gave way. Just as they were about to step inside, the mayor's phone rang. He peeked at the screen.

"Kids, I have to take this. It'll be fast. You can go in, but don't go too far. I'll be there in a minute or two."

Hannah and Nico took four cautious steps, and they were in.

6.

Goosebumps

The air was cold and thick. It smelled damp, dirty, and moldy.

And it was dark. So dark.

Downright scary.

Hannah set her backpack on the floor and zipped it open. The sound echoed in the empty space—from a corner in front, to the back wall, then along the sides. The sound came back at Hannah and Nico once, twice, and again. It gave them goosebumps.

Hannah lifted the flashlight out of her bag carefully, but still it slipped from her shaking hand and fell hard onto the floor. The friends jumped. And screamed. Their screams echoed.

It felt like the whole theater was shaking.

They looked back toward the door. Did the mayor hear them? Was he coming?

No. All they heard was scurrying—mice, probably. There had to be hundreds of them, coming out of the walls and from under the seats. Hannah and Nico were frozen in place.

Hannah felt a chilly breeze. Where was it coming from? The room was closed up. Tight. She clicked her flashlight on and shined it on the stage. It was weird. The heavy red curtain swayed slowly.

"What's moving that curtain?" Hannah asked. "There are no open windows or doors near the stage."

It would have to be a pretty big animal to make that curtain move. Or maybe a person. A crazy criminal using the Plaza as a hideout.

Nico must have been thinking the same thing, because suddenly he said, "I've seen enough. Let's go."

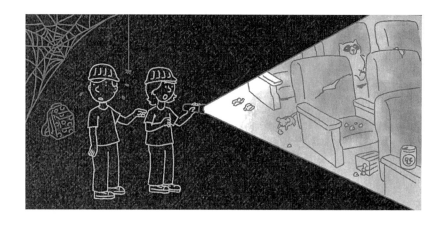

Hannah's flashlight lit up parts of the theater, one by
one, changing everything into crazy shapes. The rows of
seats became hulking bears. The box seats on the sides of
the stage seemed to be floating, attached to nothing, and
ready to fall at the slightest touch. A sign hanging over a
doorway had a single letter—a big red X—marking a place
they were definitely NOT supposed to be.

"We should go." Nico's voice was scratchy. "We
should get the mayor."

"He'll be in soon. Let's give it five minutes," said
Hannah. "Five minutes to see what we can see."

Hannah turned her flashlight toward the seats. With

slow steps and hands outreached, she found her way to a seat. She touched it. It was fuzzy and crusty at the same time. The arm was broken and hanging down. When her knee brushed it, it swung forward, then back, forward, then back. Hannah lost her balance and fell into the seat. Clouds of dust surrounded her. The seat felt like it was sucking her in deeper. She couldn't get herself out of it.

"Nico, help!" she shouted. The echo again.

Nico pulled Hannah up. They walked down the middle aisle to the back of the theater and tripped on an uneven tile. They tumbled onto the icy, filthy floor, then scrambled to their knees. When they stood up, their legs were wobbly and their hands were caked with dirt.

"Now? Can we go now?" was all Nico could say.

The echo sounded back. Nownownownownow.

Hannah grabbed Nico's hand. They raced to their backpacks, grabbed them, ran to the door, pushed it open, and hurried outside and around the back to their bikes. The autumn sun hurt their eyes.

Mayor Wilson was just hanging up. "What's it like in there?" he asked.

"Dark," Hannah answered. "Can't really see much."

"I'm going inside to take a quick look," the mayor said. "I won't be long."

The mayor grabbed a flashlight from his pocket and pulled the Stage Door open.

Hannah and Nico held their breath and waited.

"It's pretty bad," Mayor Wilson said when he returned. "We need to get the inspectors in right away. That's the only way to find out for sure if we can fix this place up. I'll call them first thing Monday morning, promise! You two have a good day."

Hannah and Nico jumped on their bikes and pedaled home. Fast.

7.
The Secret's Out

The minute Hannah and Nico got to his house, Hannah told Melissa, "We have a BIG story for the *Pilot*. It's perfect for your column."

Even though she was still in middle school, Melissa had a regular feature in the Sunday Family Section of the *Raccoon River Pilot*.

"Hmmm?" Melissa was interested.

"We're going to fix up the Plaza Theater so we can have movies, and shows, and graduations and . . ." Hannah emphasized, "*middle-school-orchestra concerts* right here in Raccoon River. Mayor Wilson is going to help."

"You are? He is?"

"Absolutely," said Hannah.

"The Plaza's been closed for years. It must be in terrible condition," Melissa said, thinking out loud. "That's a giant job."

"It is Lissa," said Nico. "We were just there. With the mayor."

"You were? How?"

"The door was open," Hannah said.

"It was? Can we get in again, so I can take some pictures?"

"It's pretty gloomy in there," said Nico.

"We can do it together," said Hannah, swallowing hard.

"Without a grown-up?"

Melissa nodded. She really wanted in on this. "I can be the grown-up. How about next weekend? The three of us. Meantime, I'll dig up some pictures of how the Plaza used to look."

Melissa brought a couple of her friends along on Saturday morning. "They can help," she explained. "Hope that's okay with you, Hannah."

Hannah was annoyed, but she said, "Good idea. Thanks, guys." The more she thought about it, the more she thought it wouldn't be bad to have extra company in the theater. Plus, three middle-schoolers were practically the same as one adult, right?

They pulled at the Stage Door. It gave way and the five of them, flashlights in hand, walked in slowly, carefully, quietly.

"Spooky," Melissa whispered.

"Major spooky," her friend Alex said.

They clicked on their flashlights. The five lights made the theater a little less scary. But it looked in even worse condition than it had last week. How were they ever going to turn this mess around?

Melissa's camera flashed on a row of chairs, on a wall lamp hanging by its wire, on the dirty red velvet curtain with its yellow fringes brushing the floor of the stage. She took some pictures in the lobby too. Flash: the falling-down candy stand. Flash: a row of rusty metal barriers with thick red rope strung through them. Flash: the ticket booth. Well, maybe the ticket booth. It was hard to tell.

"Do you really think this theater could be ready for our spring concert, Hannah? It looks pretty bad to me," said Melissa.

"I do. With enough people helping, I know we can get this place ready in time," Hannah said, starting to believe her own words.

"I hope so," said Melissa.

In between their conversations, the five kids heard scampering all around.

"Mice?" Melissa asked.

"Millions," her friend Alex teased.

This was too much for Melissa. "I've got plenty," she said, holding up her camera. "Let's go."

No one argued. When they were outside and had closed the door, Melissa said she needed one more photo: Hannah under the marquee.

Oh, the next three days were busy!

Mayor Wilson's assistant called. There was going to be a special meeting of the town council. The theater was the only subject on the agenda.

Hannah discovered that Sig Associates, the original architects of The Plaza, still had offices in the county. Sig's granddaughter Audrey was now in charge of the business.

And yes, she wanted to help restore her grandfather's building.

Melissa got a big YES too. The newspaper wanted not just one article and photos for the paper, but articles every Wednesday, right up to Valentine's Day.

Ms. Allen set aside fifteen minutes one morning for Hannah to let the class in on the big plans. Everyone volunteered. Ms. Allen said that Hannah should report on progress once a week. "Our class is going to be at the center of the action," Ms. Allen promised.

It was time for Hannah and Nico to tell their parents.

"That's a dangerous building," Hannah's mother said. "I don't want you in there."

"You're not equipped to handle a project this big." said her dad.

"You're going to need construction workers, plumbers, electricians, painters . . . "Nico's dad began.

Hannah stopped him in mid-list. "We know we can't

do this ourselves, Mr. Preston," she said. "Mayor Wilson is helping. There's a Town Council meeting next week. They'll help too."

"It's going to cost more money than I can imagine." Hannah's mother said.

"We know," said Nico.

It was hard for Hannah to listen to all of her parents' worries. Didn't they see what a good idea this was? Didn't they know how it would make Raccoon River a better place to live? Weren't they proud that their daughter had started this whole thing?

"We don't want you to get your hopes up and then be disappointed," said her mom. "No matter how hard you try and how hard everyone works, this could fail. How will you feel then?"

"I'll be sad, but I'll still be glad we tried." Hannah walked to her mother and gave her a big hug. "Besides, this won't fail. You'll see."

Melissa stepped in. "Let's wait and see what happens

after the Council meeting. And after my column runs in the *Pilot*."

The parents clinked coffee cups. "Good luck kids!"

8.

The Big Announcement

Citizens of Raccoon River,

We are about to launch our biggest restoration project ever.

Raccoon River's Plaza Theater has been closed for many years. Over that time, it has fallen into disrepair. It's up to us to bring it back to its original glory and make it home to cultural, entertainment, and social events that will enrich our lives.

This great idea started with one of our young students at Raccoon River Elementary. Our town council has enthusiastically approved the project. We have experts coming in to check the premises and let us know what work is needed.

One thing is for sure: we will need YOUR help. Watch the *Pilot* every Wednesday for photos, a progress report, and a list of things you can do.

We've put THE PLAZA PROJECT on the fast track, so, fellow citizens, please lace up your sneakers and join us!

Mayor Malcomb Wilson

Hannah and her mother read the mayor's message together at breakfast.

"Lissa took my picture in front of the theater. How come they didn't use it in the article? My name's not even there," Hannah complained.

Mom squeezed Hannah's hand gently. It wasn't much comfort.

Her mother tried again. "Maybe they'll use your photo next Wednesday."

"I didn't even know the project was approved until I read it this morning. Shouldn't *I* know before the whole world does?"

"I'm sure everyone's been very busy with this, Hannah. You saw what the mayor said. The Plaza Project is on the fast track," Mom reasoned.

"I guess," Hannah said. "The fast track means it's important, right? The fast track means the theater will be ready in time."

It was getting hard to stay angry. After all, this is what she wanted to happen.

Still, it was hard not to be disappointed that she'd been left out. Hannah knew this was a big, complicated project. She knew a lot of adults would have to be involved. But they didn't have to take it over. It was her idea. Her plan. Her theater. Well, sort of. It was supposed to be the kids who were going to make this happen.

It was starting to feel like the whole thing was getting away from her.

9.

Thumbs Up

Just one week later, there was plenty of progress to report.

```
                    THE PLAZA PROJECT
                    By Melissa Preston
                    Week 1 — October 3


        It's a GO!


        Thumbs up: The Plaza Theater may look like it's
        about to fall down, but the inspectors said it is
        sound and that repairs can begin.
        Thumbs up: Mayor Wilson appointed Jessica
        Morton as Chair of the Plaza Project. She was in
        charge of the Community Center renovation, and we all
```

know how great that turned out.

Thumbs up: Mrs. Morton has a big head start. The town council voted to put the $20,000 that we didn't use for storm cleanup this year toward theater repairs. (Hooray for the mild weather!)

Won't it be great to have our own theater! The middle-school orchestra is already signed up for a spring concert! Buy your tickets soon. (Ha!)

More next week!

THE PLAZA PROJECT

By Melissa Preston

Week 2 — October 10

Thumbs up: The plumbing team is hired. They say the tiles in the bathrooms can be saved, but they've ordered all new…um…equipment to replace the old…um… equipment.

Thumbs up: The plasterers have started. "Some of these cracks go very deep," according to Mark Burns, "but we've got it covered." Get it?

Thumbs up: With third-grader Hannah Levin in the lead (Did you know that her great uncle was Raccoon River's mayor when the Plaza was built?), the Raccoon River Kids Fund has been created. "Kids are chipping in from their allowances and taking on jobs so they can donate more," said a very happy Hannah.

THE PLAZA PROJECT

By Melissa Preston

Week 4 — October 24

Big thumbs up: The Simon family, who sponsored the new Raccoon River Medical Clinic and donated money to restock our library after the flood five years ago, has made a very generous pledge to the Plaza Theater Project. Said Mayor Wilson, "With this gift, we are almost two-thirds of the way to our goal." THANK YOU!

Thumbs up: We have toilets! (And sinks)

A message for the kids from Hannah: Next week is Halloween. Trick-or-treat for the Plaza. Ask your neighbors to chip in a dollar for the Plaza Theater when you ring their bell.

THE PLAZA PROJECT

By Melissa Preston

Week 6 — November 7

Lots of thumbs up: The interior-design committee announced the colors for the theater. All different kinds of blue. A navy-blue stage curtain with gold fringe, dark-and-light-blue checked seats, and sea-blue carpets.

A message for the kids from Hannah: Thank you to everyone. We collected $250 on Halloween. A great start. Let's get together and figure out what else we can do. Meeting at the Community Center at 10:30 this Saturday, November 12. Cookies for everyone.

Thirty-five kids showed up, from preschoolers to middle-schoolers. There were even a couple of high school kids.

"We're from the drama club," one of them told Hannah. "We figured if we helped to get the theater fixed up, we'd have a place to perform our plays."

"Makes sense, don't you think?" a second actor asked.

Were these high school students really asking Hannah, third grader, for her opinion?

"I guess," she said. Then, with more confidence, "It makes a lot of sense."

"We're in," the first actor said.

By the end of the meeting, by the time the cookies and juice were gone, the kids had a name: THE RACCOON RIVER KIDS THEATER FUND. And they had a leader.

10.
One Important Thing

What's a leader without a plan? Hannah didn't have one yet. She knew that her team of kid volunteers couldn't do the work the Plaza needed. There wasn't one of them who could replace a sink or fix a leak in the roof. They didn't know how to make a curtain or have a clue about lighting or where you go to buy 350 theater seats. Adults would do all those things.

What the kids could do was raise money. They'd proven that. The question was, could it be enough money to matter?

Maybe . . . if they picked one thing to buy. One *important* thing. But what?

"Mom, do you think I could call Mrs. Morton? I have

a question, and I'm pretty sure she'll have the answer."

"I don't see why not, Hannah."

"Really? Just call her—out of the blue?"

"Why not," Mom repeated.

"She doesn't even know me."

"She reads the paper, Hannah. She's seen your name in Melissa's articles. She knows who you are."

Mom wrote Mrs. Morton's number on a slip of paper and handed it to her. Hannah called right away—before she lost her courage.

Mrs. Morton was happy to hear from her. And she was more than willing to help the kids find a single important thing they could raise money for. There was so much the theater still needed.

"We could meet at Town Hall on Tuesday," Mrs. Morton suggested. "After school. How would that be?"

What Hannah *thought* was, "That's too soon. I have to think about this." What she *said* was, "See you Tuesday."

Mrs. Morton was waiting in Town Hall's big lobby when Hannah arrived. She had a fat, kind of sloppy loose-leaf notebook on her lap. She tapped the seat next to her on the bench, inviting Hannah to sit down.

"The whole town is buzzing about the Plaza," Mrs. Morton said. "Thank you for such a great idea, Hannah!"

"All the kids are excited too. We want to help."

Mrs. Morton handed the notebook to Hannah. "I've marked some of the pages with sticky notes. These are things the theater needs. I wrote prices on each of the flags, to help you figure out which one you think the kids can cover."

Hannah took the notebook and flipped through it. Every page was filled with photos of theater equipment and supplies with descriptions below. She turned to the page marked with the first sticky note. Yikes! She couldn't believe how much a stage curtain cost. Tile for the lobby floor was way out of reach too. Carpeting for the aisles was possible at $1,500. (Not much fun, though.) Seat number plaques cost $900. The very best of the popcorn poppers was $600.

(That sounded delicious, but not important enough.) On the next page, a concession stand with a freezer for ice-cream treats was $2,000. (It came with a free first fill-up—a selection of your choice—the description said.)

"Mrs. Morton," Hannah said to get her attention. "I found two things." Hannah pointed to them.

"Great choices, Hannah. A perfect contribution from the children."

"I don't know if we can do both. It's not up to me. All the kids should decide. Can I tell you next week?"

"Of course. Thank you."

As she walked toward the exit, Hannah noticed a bulletin board hanging near the elevators. The headline said, RACOON RIVER IS PROUD. Below there was a photograph of Caitlin Collins, one of music's most popular stars. She'd won the TV Talent Search a few years ago, and now she was going to have her own TV series. But Caitlin didn't live here. As far as Hannah knew, she never did. Hannah couldn't imagine why Raccoon River was proud of her.

Hmmmm?

THE PLAZA PROJECT

By Melissa Preston

Sticky Thumbs Up: The Raccoon River Kids voted to use the funds they raise to purchase a concession stand (with ice-cream freezer) and a top-of-the line popcorn popper. (They also get to pick the candy for the first fill-up. Yum!)

Meanwhile, *lots* of work was going on at the Plaza . . .

11.
THE BIG PUSH

Two-thousand six-hundred dollars. Now *that* was big. That was important. Popcorn was important. Candy was important. Absolutely.

But how were the kids going to raise that kind of money? In only three months.

Hannah made a new list to share at their next meeting.

Little Kids:

1. Art show at the library with paid admission, sell pictures too

2. Lemonade/snack stands at school plays, dance performances, gymnastics meets

Middle Kids:

1. Leaf raking

2. Odd jobs at home

3. Old books and toys garage sales

Middle School:

1. Car washes

2. Dog walking and cat sitting

3. Babysitting

High School:

1. Garage and shed clean-ups

2. Snow shoveling

3. Organize holiday activities for kids

All the kids were eager to get started—all except Brandon Big Mouth. He thought the whole thing was impossible.

"The theater is so lame," he announced. "There's no way it can get fixed up enough to use it. Did anyone really look at it? It's going to fall down if more than ten people go inside. I sure won't be one of them."

AND "Do you know how much 2,600 dollars is? It is

A LOT. It's more than a bunch of kids can earn."

AND "If I get any money, I'm not going to throw it away on this theater."

AND "I heard the theater was haunted. No one will go to a haunted theater."

A few kids started to worry. They called out their questions. "Is it safe for us to go inside?" "Are there spiders?" "Or rats?" "Will any big stars want to do shows there?" "What if it IS haunted?"

One by one, Hannah answered them. For the last question, she said, "So what if it is haunted?" Hannah put her hands on her hips. "It might be."

That got the group's attention.

"Nico and I went there. It was pretty spooky. The weirdest thing was that stuff was moving. There were no windows or open doors, but things were swaying. There were sounds too. It *could* have been ghosts." Hannah paused. "Probably not, though."

All Brandon could say to that was, "See? I told you!"

Someone yelled out, "Are you afraid of a few ghosts, Brandon?"

The rest of the kids started to talk about what they would do to help.

The Raccoon River Kids dug in. Most of the time, things went the way they were supposed to, and bit by bit the money added up.

There *were* a few unexpected moments.

Like the day Lili, the youngest (and the spunkiest) volunteer, made the lemonade for her stand at a gymnastics meet herself. She did exactly what she had watched her mother do all those other times. Except that she forgot one little ingredient—the sugar. Her customers got a surprise when they took a sip. SOUR! But they came back the next time Lili had a stand. After all, it was for the Plaza.

Or the day Brady decided to make *healthy* cupcakes instead of everyone's favorites to sell at his father's bakery. These new cupcakes were whole wheat/oatmeal/flax with raisins. "Not a bad muffin," one customer said, "but not much of a cupcake." Still, Brady's customers came back for more. Because it was all for the Plaza.

And there was Melissa's Photo Stand. Everyone in Raccoon River knew Melissa was a good photographer, so when she set up a snap-shot studio at the library, lots of people came.

"An early start on our holiday cards," Mrs. Morton said as she arranged her children into a pose.

That evening, Melissa carefully put the photographic paper into her printer and gently pulled the memory card out of her camera. But her hand hit a glass of milk that spilled all over the table and wrecked the card. The photos were ruined. That meant lots of families with no holiday-card photos and no money for Melissa to contribute to the Plaza fund.

What was worse, she had already practically promised the middle school orchestra that they could hold the spring concert at the Plaza. Melissa would just have to set up her photo shop again. Would her customers return? Yes, they did. After all, it was for the Plaza.

They were five weeks into the Big Push. *All* those kids chipping in a part of their allowances, *all* those cupcakes and glasses of lemonade and raked leaves, clean cars and organized garages. *All* those kids working hard at *all* those jobs had contributed more than $900 to the Raccoon River Kids Plaza Fund. It was a lot of money . . .

Just not enough.

12.

We Need More

Hannah knew that unless something big happened, there was no way they were going to reach the magic number: $2,600. What they needed was a fresh idea, and it was up to Hannah to come up with it.

Some charities had collection cans in stores, so people could put their change into them. The kids could decorate some old cans and ask stores to put them on their counters. That could help. But it probably wasn't going to make a big difference.

Some charities made phone calls or sent post cards asking people to make donations.

They could try it. But Hannah's mother shot that

down. "You can't bother people that way, Hannah. That's not going to raise money. It's going to make people annoyed."

"I've run out of ideas," Hannah confessed.

Just as she said those words, Hannah noticed the headline on the *Pilot's* sports page.

```
Frank Green scores five three-point
        shots five games in a row.
```

This could be her answer. Frank Green grew up here. He might be playing basketball for the Houston Rockets now, but he and his success started in Raccoon River. He was coached by Raccoon River High's winningest-ever athletic director. Coach Jeff had led his teams—basketball, baseball, and football—to state championships for many years.

Frank Green owes a lot to the town, Hannah thought. *And I bet he knows it! He's the guy who can help us raise money.*

Now she just had to figure out how.

It was Saturday. Hannah and her mom were heading to the mall in search of a birthday gift for Hannah's grandma. Mom was wearing an old college-concert T-shirt that was so faded you could hardly read the words. A couple of guys in the band had signed the shirt. If you looked really closely you could almost read their autographs.

Hannah was still thinking about how Frank Green could help them raise money for the Plaza. The pieces started to come together.

A T-shirt.

A famous basketball hero.

An autograph.

Hannah had her answer. All that was left to do was contact Frank Green.

She thought of Mr. Collins, who owned the sports

shop at the mall. He had helped Nico with his blueberry project. He probably knew Frank Green and could help her reach him.

Mr. Collins was behind the counter when Hannah got to his store. He greeted her with his usual, "What's up?"

Hannah was about to tell him about the headline in the newspaper and how she needed to get in touch with Frank Green and how she hoped Mr. Collins could help with that. But she was distracted by a poster hanging above the counter. It was the same poster—for Caitlin Collins's music tour—that Hannah had seen in Town Hall. Why did Mr. Collins have it in his shop?

"Hello," Hannah started. Then she blurted out, "How come you have a sign for a music concert in your store?"

Mr. Collins turned around to look at the poster. "Oh. My niece sent it to me, so I figured I'd hang it. I'm very proud of her." He pointed to the autograph. Hannah couldn't read it from where she was standing, so Mr. Collins read it aloud. "For my favorite uncle. Thank you for giving me my first real gig."

Of course! Caitlin COLLINS. Mr. COLLINS. COLLINS Sports.

"You're kidding. I mean, you're kidding, right?" Hannah took a breath. "I didn't know you were related to Caitlin. I mean THE Caitlin."

"I thought everyone in Raccoon River knew," Mr. Collins answered.

"Maybe everyone but me. What does she mean about her first gig?"

"She's making an inside joke! Years ago, Caitlin and her dad lived with me for about two years while her mother was working on a special project at a university in Argentina. Caitlin and I decided to make a commercial for local TV. We wrote a song about sports and how our store has everything you need. Caitlin starred in it. She was nine, maybe ten. And talented."

"You're kidding."

Mr. Collins was almost laughing. He shook his head.

"You're not kidding. You really are Caitlin Collins's uncle."

"I am," Mr. Collins said. "And I think I have a copy of that commercial here. Would you like to watch it?"

"Would I!"

Mr. Collins slipped a CD into his computer and turned the screen around so Hannah could see it. A little girl was standing at the front of Collins Sports. Was that Caitlin? Caitlin the superstar? She was much younger, but yes, she looked like Caitlin, she sounded like Caitlin.

"That's amazing."

"And fun to see again. But that's not why you stopped by, is it?" Mr. Collins asked.

It took a full minute for Hannah to recover. "No, that's not why I'm here. I was hoping you had a way to get in touch with Frank Green. I think he can help us raise some money for the Plaza Project."

"Are you going to ask him to sign some shirts for you? You can probably sell them for $20 or $25."

Hannah nodded.

Mr. Collins gave her Frank Green's email address.

THE PLAZA PROJECT
By Melissa Preston
WEEK 12 — December 19

News from the kids: Our Basketball Hero Frank Green has signed a dozen Rockets T-shirts for us to sell. $25 each. (Frank's team donated the shirts, and Frank signed them in honor of Coach Jeff.) Contact the email address below if you're interested.

They sold all twelve shirts. $300 dollars for the fund.

At their next meeting, someone in the group, a fifth grader, Hannah thought, raised her hand and said, "My dad is always talking about a football player who grew up here. I think he's retired, but he was pretty famous. Maybe he'll sign some shirts for us."

Someone else knew that there was a baseball player on some pro team who had been a star player at Raccoon River High.

"Let's try to find them. If it works," Hannah said, "this could really add up."

Everyone cheered!

But Hannah was thinking bigger thoughts . . .

13.

The January Thaw

It could not be. Not yet! Even if the weather guy on TV kept talking about it.

It was the January thaw, and it was here. Every year, around the middle of January, the temperatures rose, the snow melted, scarves and gloves got a rest. Hannah had been trying to ignore the calendar, but she could not ignore this. Valentine's Day was getting close.

There were less than four weeks to go. The Kids' Plaza Fund was stuck at $1,647.52. At the rate they were going, even if they sold a dozen more T-shirts, two dozen more T-shirts, it didn't look like they could come up with a thousand dollars in four weeks.

Or could they?

Hannah had tried not to think about Caitlin Collins. It wouldn't be fair to ask her for money just out of the blue like that. People probably asked her for all kinds of stuff all the time.

It had to be annoying.

Of course, she was The Number One Music Star in the Entire World. She had lots of money. And she had lived in Raccoon River for a couple of years. Her uncle still did. He might have told her about the Plaza Project. She probably wanted to help, but no one had asked her.

One thing was for sure. If Caitlin Collins stepped in, it would put the kids over the top.

Hannah told her idea, her last hope, to Nico and Melissa. The three of them sat in front of the big window in the living room, watching icicles drip.

"We need another thousand dollars to pay for the popper and the candy stand."

Melissa asked, "Could we just buy one of them? Do

we have enough money for the concession stand?"

"Not yet. But we could probably raise enough for that before the opening."

"We can always buy the popcorn maker later," Nico offered.

"We could," Hannah agreed, but her face told a different story. She wouldn't be satisfied unless the kids kept their promise—their whole promise—and on time!

"I was thinking," said Hannah, "we could ask Caitlin Collins to help us."

"Yeah, right." Melissa said.

"Why Caitlin Collins?" Nico asked.

"Because she is Mr. Collins's niece."

"She is?"

"Yup."

"And because she lived in Raccoon River and went to our school for two years.

And because when she lived here, she probably wished she had a place to perform, but the Plaza was closed even then."

Melissa and Nico thought about that for a while.

Finally, Melissa said, "It's worth a shot."

"Our best shot," Nico said. "I bet she'll donate a thousand dollars easy."

"We are talking about a theater, though," Melissa said. "You know...where they have concerts."

"Concerts. C O N C E R T S! Thanks, Lissa," Hannah said.

Hannah's brain was working overtime. Maybe... maybe Caitlin would perform at the Plaza. Maybe...maybe she would be the star of the very first event there. Maybe... maybe she would give the money from the tickets to the theater fund.

Lots of super-stars did stuff like that.

Hannah rang Mr. Collins's doorbell. "I would have

been so disappointed if you hadn't come by," he said when he opened the door.

That took Hannah by surprise. "Huh?" was all she could think of to say.

"I figure if I were you, I'd be ringing my doorbell. If I were you, I'd be thinking that Caitlin Collins can help raise money for the Plaza. If I were you, I'd be hoping that that nice Mr. Collins might call Caitlin for me."

Hannah still wasn't sure what to say. So, she just stepped closer to Mr. Collins and gave him a big hug.

Mr. Collins patted her head. "Your timing is perfect. Caitlin and I video-chat once a month, and today's the day. She should be calling in about a half hour. How about a glass of milk while we wait?"

"Today? You mean I'm going to talk to Caitlin Collins face-to-face? Today?"

"That's exactly what I mean."

The tablet on Mr. Collins's kitchen table rang. He and Caitlin talked for a while. Then he gave Hannah his chair, right in front of the screen, and introduced her to Caitlin.

She looked just like she did in her posters and on TV and on the covers of magazines.

She was so nice, so easy to talk to, not one bit stuck up.

Her voice was kind of scratchy, though. She was sipping a drink from a big mug of something steamy. Her throat was always tired the morning after a concert, she explained. Hannah shouldn't worry. She was fine, and she'd be in her best voice on Valentine's Day when she would perform at the Plaza.

Hannah wasn't sure she'd heard Caitlin right. "How did you know?"

"My uncle might have mentioned something," Caitlin said, winking. "Let me know who will be calling my manager so we can set this all up. My uncle has the number."

Hannah and Caitlin talked for a few minutes. As they were hanging up, Caitlin said, "See you February 14."

"Absolutely!"

14.
Here's How

Hannah practiced how she was going to tell the kids the good news at their Saturday meeting. She was bursting, but she waited until they gave Mrs. Morton the money they had collected that week, until Mrs. Morton added it up and announced their new total, and until they all felt disappointed and worried.

That's when Hannah stood up.

"That's great."

"But, but, but we have so little time left before Valentine's Day, and we still need . . ."

Brady paused, calculating how much more they needed.

"Nearly $1,000," Mrs. Morton said. "But don't fret. You should all be very proud of yourselves. You got really close to your goal. No one expected you to actually raise $2,600.

No one expected you to be able to purchase the popcorn popper and the concession stand."

"*We* did," Hannah said. "*We* expected to. And we will."

The kids cheered.

When everyone had settled down, Zoe said very softy, "How?"

"Here's how," Hannah said. "Caitlin Collins is going to help."

The kids said nothing.

Hannah kept on talking. She filled everyone in on how Caitlin was Mr. Collins's niece (Did you know that?), and how she lived in Raccoon River for two years and went to Raccoon River Elementary (Did you know that?), and how Hannah had video-chatted with her (Really!), and how

Caitlin Collins agreed to be the first performer at the Plaza on Valentine's Day.

Absolutely.

Still silence. So, Hannah went on. "All we have to do is sell tickets. Caitlin is giving the money from the ticket sales to our fund. There's some stuff—like microphones and people to work the lights and the curtain—that we have to pay for. All the rest is for the fund."

Still no one said a word. Even Hannah had run out of them.

Then, one by one, the children began to clap and shout and laugh out loud and stamp their feet and cheer. The sound built slowly, steadily, until it filled the whole room and wrapped around every kid.

When it got quiet again, Hannah told them, "There's more."

"More?" someone shouted.

"Yup. Each of us gets two free tickets. In special reserved seats."

Another roar and applause. Hannah held up her hands. Everyone settled down.

"We have a lot to do." Hannah took out her red-and-white polka-dot notebook. "I have a list."

Nico stood up. "Of course you do!"

Hannah had started to read the long list of what had to happen next, when she heard a familiar voice shout out.

"Hold on!"

It was Brandon. Brandon, who had not lifted a pinky to help them raise money. Brandon, who had not contributed even a dime from his allowance. The same Brandon who had poked fun at almost every effort the kids made.

Hannah didn't want to start an argument. Why ruin the great feeling? She decided to pretend that Brandon hadn't said anything. She continued to read her list.

"Hold on," Brandon repeated, a little louder. "You need to sell the tickets in advance if you're going to have the candy stand and popcorn maker on opening night. That isn't easy. You have to know what you're doing."

"We are getting help from a lot of people," Hannah said.

"I have experience," Brandon said.

Mrs. Morton stepped in. "Why don't you and Brandon talk about this later? We have to end the meeting now. Some of the parents are already arriving to pick up their children."

Brandon nodded. Hannah nodded.

Zoe asked, "Is this a secret, or can we tell people about Caitlin Collins?"

Hannah told her, "Tell everyone. We want to sell every single ticket!"

Brandon stayed behind. He told Hannah, "I really do have experience with selling tickets. My dad worked for a company that set up shows all over the country. He had to travel a lot. In summers, he used to take me with him. While he was doing things, I would help in ticket booths all over the towns. We'd set them up in the morning and keep them open all day. Then set up in another place the next day. That could work for us here."

Us? Hannah was thinking. But maybe Brandon did have experience that could help. "Do you think you and your dad could lend a hand?" Hannah asked.

"My dad's not home anymore. He and my mom . . . well . . . they . . . I mean, he left."

For the second time that day, Hannah had no words.

"It's okay. We're doing okay," Brandon said softly.

"I didn't know," said Hannah. "I guess that's why you couldn't be a part of our fund raising."

Brandon hung his head down and nodded.

Hannah quickly added, "It would be great if you could help us with ticket sales. If you have time, we sure could use your experience."

Brandon looked up. "I'll do my best."

15.

Opening Night

By February 5th every ticket for the Caitlin Collins Concert at the Plaza Theater was gone.

That meant:

350 seats minus 100 seats given away to the Raccoon River Kids and other important people = 250 paid-for tickets.

250 paid-for tickets times $35 = $8,750

$8,750 minus $3,287 of expenses = $5,463

Five-thousand, four-hundred and sixty-three dollars!

Plus, the money the Kids Fund had raised before the concert was announced = $7,063, more or less

A WHOLE LOT MORE THAN $2,600!

On February 7th, one week before the big opening, the popcorn machine and concession stand were delivered. Mrs. Morton invited all the kids to the theater after school to celebrate their contribution. She picked a couple of middle-school kids to plug them in.

Everyone counted down:

TEN, NINE, EIGHT, SEVEN, SIX, FIVE, FOUR, THREE, TWO, ONE

The lights went on. The freezer in the concession stand started humming. The kids stared in silence for a moment and then burst out in cheers, high-fiving each other and shouting,

"We did it, WE did it, we REALLY did it!"

Melissa caught the moment with a great photo that made page 1 of the *Pilot*.

By the weekend before Valentine's Day, the Plaza Theater was ready, right down to the shiny buttons on the ushers' vests.

When Hannah arrived on Valentine's night with her parents and her best friend Nico, they were led to four seats in the center of the auditorium.

"These say reserved," Hannah told the usher.

"Uh-huh," she said. "They *are* reserved—for you."

They scooted through the row to their seats.

"What are these?" Nico asked, pointing to plaques on the arms of each of the four seats.

The person sitting right in front of the Levin family turned around.

Mayor Wilson smiled. "Let me read it to you. *With thanks to Hannah Levin, who took the lead and gave us back our theater.*"

"Really?" Hannah whispered.

"Yes. These are your seats. Whenever any of you buy tickets at the Plaza, you will get these seats. They come with the best wishes of everyone in Raccoon River."

Hannah leaned over to Nico. "This is nice. They didn't make a big deal about it. I wouldn't like it if there were speeches and stuff."

Caitlin Collins and her band were the best. They sang all their hit songs with lots of people in the audience singing and dancing along. At the end of the concert, the band left the stage and Caitlin returned alone with her guitar.

"I have a new song that I wrote just for today. It's dedicated to everyone in Raccoon River, but especially to the Kids. You proved that a great idea, dedication, and hard work can make a real difference. I applaud you."

The song was beautiful, and the chorus was catchy. By the third time it came around, everyone was standing, applauding, and singing.

When the audience sat down, Mayor Wilson called out from his seat.

"One more thing, Ms. Collins," he said.

Caitlin waited on stage.

Five of the Raccoon River Kids walked to the stage. Lili was up front, holding a bunch of flowers. She handed them to Caitlin. The audience stood and called out, "Bravo! Bravo!"

In the midst of the applause, one boy—it was

Brandon—walked up the steps to the stage holding more flowers. He whispered to Caitlin. She leaned into the microphone and said, "Hannah Levin, please join us here."

Hannah hesitated. Mayor Wilson turned around. "It's your turn, Hannah."

Up on stage, Brandon gave Hannah the flowers. She choked out a thank you into the microphone. Then added, "We did it together. All of us."

Brandon stepped back, looking Hannah in the eyes. He mouthed the words, "Thank you." And something else. Hannah wasn't sure what he was trying to say, but it kind of looked like, "What's next?"

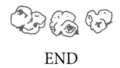

END

5